THE
GENTLE
GIANT

BY
MIKE PILCHER

ILLUSTRATIONS BY
PAT ALLEN AND MASON PILCHER

To order additional copies of this book, contact:
Xlibris
844-714-8691
www.Xlibris.com
Orders@Xlibris.com

ISBN: Softcover   978-1-6641-5028-7
         Hardcover   978-1-6641-5029-4
         EBook   978-1-6641-5027-0

Library of Congress Control Number: 2020925897

Print information available on the last page.

Rev. date: 04/27/2021

A Children's book dedicated to the life of a four-legged best friend. He was our best friend. He loved his family as much as we loved him.

Jackson was my Black Labrador Retriever. When we first met, he was only eight weeks old. He had a big family -- ten other brothers and sisters! They were all looking for a good home. There was just something about him that stood out. I chose him and he chose me.

While Jackson's brothers and sisters ran around doing what puppies do, Jackson would sit by his food bowl. He was watching and patiently waiting for his next meal. Jackson was always the first puppy in his family to eat. That never changed.

Jackson loved being loved. When he got a good belly scratch or behind the ear rub, Jackson would make sounds like he was saying "thank you" in dog language.

Jackson could be a "little" mischievous. He loved to chew on lots of shoes and dug lots of holes. He also tore up a lot of things he should not have and even went swimming where he should not have.

Jackson loved to swim. One day, on our way to the lake, he got so excited to swim he jumped out of my truck too early. He tumbled and rolled to a stop in the parking lot. I thought he might be hurt. Before I could park the truck, he was splashing in the water.

Jackson also loved to eat. Every morning and every evening Jackson would sit by his bowl when it was time to eat. He would stare at me with his big brown eyes until I put that cup of food in his bowl. Jackson would kiss me first and then lick his bowl clean.

With all the eating Jackson loved to do, he grew bigger and bigger and bigger.

Jackson grew up fast. He grew from the size of a big watermelon to a small refrigerator in about three years.

Jackson grew so big that some grown ups were afraid of him.

But, the children he met would take one look into those big brown eyes, see that big black tail wagging and know he was just a puppy dog spirit in a big dog body. Children always saw the love Jackson wanted to give them and Jackson always knew the love he wanted to give them.

Jackson was also very smart and he loved to explore. He learned how to escape from a doggy fence in our yard. It was not easy.

He had to pull a latch off of a gate with his teeth, nudge the gate with his paw and go!

Jackson was a free spirit. He would run across the street and play in the creek for hours. I could always tell he had a great day by how muddy he was.

When I would come home from work and there was no Jackson, I would whistle for him. No matter where he was or what he was doing, he heard my whistle. As soon as he heard that whistle, I could hear him coming home.

That whistle meant three things to Jackson.

Daddy was home.

It's time to eat.

Daddy's going to scratch my belly...after I eat!

Jackson was really comfortable with his Pack, his family. Then, came our son, Mason. Jackson was used to getting all of the attention. We now welcomed a new member to our Pack.

The day we brought Mason home, Jackson was anxiously excited. He didn't know what to think of this new member to our Pack, but he was excited.

Jackson was so excited! He could not stop wagging his tail. He knew having a new member of the Pack was a super good thing.

Jackson was always ready to walk in the middle of the night with me when baby Mason needed to walk just to get back to sleep.

Big Jackson loved little Mason. Jackson's big kisses made Mason laugh and laugh.

Mason couldn't play the same games Jackson was used to, like fetch or chase. So, one day, we pretended Jackson was a horse and little Mason was a cowboy.

Jackson lay down and Mason crawled on his back. Jackson, the gentle giant, lay still while Mason sat and played on his back. Jackson knew that little guy on his back was part of our Pack.

Jackson was a huge, slobbering, loveable, giant mess! He was my mess and then our mess.

Jackson was a wonderful, loving, free-spirited, four-legged, gentle giant that was more than a dog. He was my friend. He was my best friend. He was our best friend.

Printed in the United States
by Baker & Taylor Publisher Services